SPOTLIGHT ON THE CIVIL RIGHTS MOVEMENT™

THE BLACK POWER MOVEMENT AND CIVIL UNREST

KERRY HINTON

Rosen YA™
New York

Published in 2018 by The Rosen Publishing Group, Inc.
29 East 21st Street, New York, NY 10010

First Edition

Library of Congress Cataloging-in-Publication Data

Names: Hinton, Kerry, author.
Title: The black power movement and civil unrest / Kerry Hinton.
Description: New York : Rosen Publishing, 2018 | Series: Spotlight on the civil rights movement | Includes bibliographical references and index. | Audience: Grades 5–10.
Identifiers: LCCN 2017017485| ISBN 9781538380178 (library bound) | ISBN 9781538380161 (pbk.) | ISBN 9781538380185 (6 pack)
Subjects: LCSH: African Americans—Civil rights—History—20th century—Juvenile literature. | Black power—United States—History—20th century—Juvenile literature. | Civil rights movements—United States—History—20th century—Juvenile literature. | African Americans—Politics and government—20th century—Juvenile literature. | United States—Race relations—Juvenile literature.
Classification: LCC E185.61 .H658 2017 | DDC 323.1196/0730904—dc23
LC record available at https://lccn.loc.gov/2017017485

Manufactured in the United States of America

On the cover: Scenes of protest marches, slogans of black pride, and an impatience with the slow process of equal civil rights for the black community were hallmarks of 1960s America.

CONTENTS

BEFORE BLACK POWER: THE CIVIL RIGHTS MOVEMENT

Life for African Americans in the first half of the twentieth century was difficult. Slavery had been abolished by the passage of the Thirteenth Amendment in 1865, but enforcing the law proved difficult. Without enforcement, many southern states passed legislation known as Jim Crow laws that limited the freedoms of black Americans. Under Jim Crow, African Americans in the South were segregated from white society and considered second-class citizens. They were forced to use separate entrances to buildings and buses and were not even allowed to share the same public parks and pools as whites. In the early 1960s, the civil rights movement changed much of this. Sit-ins, boycotts, and other peaceful protests helped lead

During the Jim Crow era, segregation was so common that it was accepted as an unchanging fact of life for many people in the South.

to the passage of the Civil Rights Act of 1964. This law made discrimination based on race, color, religion, gender, or national origin illegal. It also ended segregation in public places and schools.

THE TWILIGHT OF THE CIVIL RIGHTS MOVEMENT

Although the progress of the civil rights movement was impressive, racism and violence against blacks and civil rights supporters increased after the Civil Rights Act of 1964 became law. Between 1964 and 1968, riots, assassinations, and police brutality became even more common than before. Younger activists felt that sit-ins and protests would not be enough to truly change society. This viewpoint continued to grow, especially following the assassination of Dr. Martin Luther King Jr. in 1968. The violent murder of a preacher who spoke only of peaceful means of integration and achieving justice was shocking. The Declaration of Independence stated that all men "are created equal" and deserve the right to "Life, Liberty, and the Pursuit of Happiness," but this seemed like a

The age of nonviolent protest began to fade in the mid-1960s, largely due to the violence peaceful protesters experienced at the hands of law enforcement.

hollow promise. Many younger activists at this time refused to rely on the white community to grant them more rights and power—they wanted control over their own lives and futures. To do that, they felt they needed to separate themselves.

THE NATION OF ISLAM

The idea of self-segregation for blacks was not new. Some black leaders had been promoting the idea of a Back to Africa movement as early as the early 1800s, believing that freed slaves would never be on equal footing with whites. The formation of the Nation of Islam in 1930 was another link in this chain. The Nation of Islam combined the religion of Islam with the politics of segregation. Elijah Muhammad, its second leader, taught his followers (known as Black Muslims) self-reliance and self-determination to help them live life without the help of white America. The membership of the Nation of Islam swelled from five hundred in 1952 to thirty thousand in 1963. Part of this increase was due to the work of Malcolm X, a close advisor to Elijah Muhammad and the Nation of Islam's spokesman during those years. The racial pride and self-sufficiency promoted by the Nation of Islam influenced the activists who would later make up the Black Power movement.

Elijah Muhammad took a small religious and political movement with a very low profile in the 1930s to one with international recognition by the early 1960s.

MALCOLM X

Malcolm Little was a thief who was sentenced to ten years in prison for burglary in 1946. There, he decided to change his life. He read constantly, converted to Islam, and after meeting Elijah Muhammad, changed his name to Malcolm X. He chose X as a rejection of white society. As the Nation of Islam's spokesman, he preached against white society and the "blue-eyed devils" responsible for the oppression of blacks. He also defended the use of violence against whites as self-defense. These ideas are at the core of black nationalism. In 1963, Malcolm left the Nation of Islam. After a trip to Saudi Arabia in 1964, Malcolm's values began to evolve. As he saw people of all races worshipping in the capital of Islam, he

After leaving the Nation of Islam, Malcolm X softened his views of Black Nationalism. He later changed his name to Al-Hajj Malik El-Shabazz.

embraced the idea of multiculturalism. He planned to take the battle for equality worldwide, but he was assassinated in 1965 by three members of the Nation of Islam in Harlem, New York City.

URBAN CONDITIONS

During the Great Migration (1916–1970), many African Americans moved north to escape segregation and the low wages of the South. Northern cities had more industry, and there was more potential to live better lives. Upon arriving, however, African Americans found that discrimination still existed, even though it was not written into law. Job opportunities, education, and income for them were all well below the standard enjoyed by white Americans. The quality and safety of housing was also a problem. Landlords in nicer neighborhoods refused to rent to African Americans, and many whites refused to live in the same neighborhoods. Some whites left cities completely as more people of color moved in. Many banks refused loans to African

Slums like this one in Baltimore became increasingly common during the 1960s. These neighborhoods often lacked employment opportunities and proper social services.

Americans, which kept them trapped by poverty. As a result, many blacks were forced to live together in poor neighborhoods called ghettos or slums. Ghetto life offered little opportunity for better lives for black Americans.

CIVIL UNREST

The poor urban conditions many blacks experienced were directly linked to violence in cities. During the 1960s, riots crippled New York, Detroit, Los Angeles, and other cities across the country. The year 1967 saw more of this violence than ever before. During what was called the long hot summer of 1967, 159 riots lasting days erupted in cities. That year, President Johnson appointed the Kerner Commission to look into the cause of this violence and how to prevent it from happening in the future. They determined the cause was racism. In their words, America was "moving toward two societies—one black, one white, separate and unequal." Police

Although the Kerner Commission recommended job training and better housing for people living in slums, President Johnson dismissed their findings.

brutality was a major factor in these riots. In many cases, police overreacted to peaceful protests against the unjust deaths of African Americans. The use of police dogs, fire hoses, and unjustified violence pushed many blacks to respond with violence themselves.

THE ROOTS OF BLACK POWER

The formation of the Student Nonviolent Coordinating Committee (SNCC) was another step toward the birth of the Black Power movement. SNCC was instrumental in attracting white and black college students to join the marches, sit-ins, and protests of the early 1960s. By 1965, a new generation of activists was exploring different ideas about how to obtain equal rights for people of color. This changing mindset was strengthened by the 1966 shooting of James Meredith during his peaceful solo March Against Fear in Mississippi. Meredith had also been the first African American to enroll at the University of Mississippi in 1962 following the Supreme Court's *Brown v. Board of Education* decision.

The artwork of the Civil Rights Era was powerful. It often tried to remind Americans that the people in search of fair treatment were the same as the rest of their countrymen.

Meredith's shooting—from which he later recovered—seemed like a rejection of progress to many people. Awful living conditions and continued violence at the hands of police and hate groups like the Ku Klux Klan (KKK) convinced more and more activists that a new approach was needed: Black Power.

This term was first used by SNCC's president Stokely Carmichael in 1966 at a speech in Mississippi at a rally for James Meredith. Carmichael questioned the usefulness of nonviolent protest in achieving equality. Not everyone agreed with his ideas—Martin Luther King Jr. and many other black leaders still believed that nonviolence was the best way to level the playing field for African Americans.

Black Power sought to improve the reality of black life in the 1960s by adopting the ideas of black nationalism previously supported by the Nation of Islam, Malcolm X, and others. Separation from white society began to make more and more sense to some blacks. In their eyes, nonviolence would only take African Americans so far. Things were better in some ways, but blacks were still far behind whites economically and politically. Integration alone was proving insufficient—a readjustment of the power structure was needed.

Under chairman Stokely Carmichael, the ideas of SNCC began to change in the face of increasing violence toward blacks despite the legal advances of the early 1960s.

THE BLACK POWER MOVEMENT

Black Power meant different things to different people. It also showed that the American black community was not one large group with one mind. Some Black Power groups still desired integration but with the same fairness and opportunities as white Americans. Some Black Power groups wanted complete separation from the larger society and were willing to make that happen even if it led to an armed revolution. Many organizations were inspired by Malcolm X and revolutionary leaders who were fighting oppression around the world. Almost all groups did agree on one thing: self-defense against violent oppression.

Most older members of the civil rights movement who still supported nonviolence did not agree with this strategy. To them, the message of Black Power could undo all of the accomplishments

The closed, raised fist became the universal symbol of the Black Power movement. For many, it represented resistance in the face of oppressive laws in an unjust system.

of the past. Despite Black Power's positive aspects, much of white society saw the Black Power movement only as angry and violent. Critics of the movement rarely asked themselves why this anger and violence still existed.

In the 1960s, the afro was one of the most visible symbols of the black community's embrace of its African heritage. Along with the music of the era, it represented cultural pride and a sense of self-worth.

Black Power was also a demonstration of racial pride and strength. This attitude was reflected in the music, art, and fashions of the time. The soul singer James Brown urged African Americans to "say it loud—I'm black and I'm proud!" Instead of using chemicals to make their hair straight, like white hair, young black men and women popularized hairstyles like the Afro and cornrows. Black films and art began to reach a larger audience. Since whites and blacks had been segregated for so many years, it was the first time that many whites saw what black Americans actually valued and thought. This pride was also demonstrated in American English. The word "negro" was discarded and replaced by "black" and "Afro-American." "Black is beautiful" became a popular phrase.

THE BLACK PANTHERS

One of the best-known groups of the Black Power movement was the Black Panthers. The Black Panther Party for Self-Defense was founded in 1966 in Oakland, California. Bobby Seale and Huey Newton, two college students, had decided to legally combat the police brutality they saw in their neighborhood. At the time, California had an open-carry gun law, which allowed gun owners to have loaded firearms in public. The Panthers took advantage of the law and started patrols to "police the police." They would travel through their neighborhoods with cameras and law books to make sure police stops were lawful.

After the Black Panthers arrived with weapons at the state capitol in Sacramento, they were allowed to keep them since it was within the scope of the law and they were not disturbing the peace.

Even though they weren't breaking any laws, these patrols disturbed the law enforcement community. Almost immediately after the patrols began, the California legislature tried to pass the Mulford Act, which would put an end to the state's open-carry law. In response, thirty armed members of the group gathered to peacefully protest at the state assembly in Sacramento, California, in 1967.

Bobby Seale, the chairman of the Black Panther Party, read a statement against the proposed law and police brutality. The protesters were then arrested. One result of this event was increased national exposure for the Black Panthers and their message. Membership began to increase over the next few years.

Soon after this, they developed a Ten-Point Program that outlined their goals. They demanded full employment, equal housing, and control for black America of its own destiny. These goals echoed the desires of both Malcolm X and the civil rights movement in general. Like Malcolm X, the Black Panthers were militant, meaning that they believed in using violence for self-defense. Some Americans accused members of the movement of fighting racism with racism, but contrary to popular belief, the Black Panthers were not antiwhite. They were against a system that favored whites. They wanted all ethnic groups, women, and the working class to be free from poverty and injustice.

Bobby Seale spent four years in prison for contempt of court from 1968 to 1972. After his release, he ran for the office of mayor of Oakland, California, but lost to his opponent.

OPPOSITION TO BLACK POWER

Some of the strongest voices against Black Power came from African Americans. The Southern Christian Leadership Conference (SCLC) and the National Association for the Advancement of Colored People (NAACP) both opposed the term "Black Power," as well as the movement's message and its goals. Many African Americans supported nonviolence as a means to improving life for their communities and were fearful that the ideas of Black Power would only bring more violence against blacks.

The US government was also very concerned with the violence advocated by some of the more militant members of the Black Power movement. In 1967, the Federal Bureau of Investigation (FBI) began to use its Counterintelligence Program (COINTELPRO) to investigate and infiltrate Black Power groups.

The mission of COINTELPRO was to "expose, disrupt...or otherwise neutralize the activities of the Black nationalists." Many in the government feared the idea of a leader who could unite and possibly arm the black community. Making the Black Panthers look bad would reduce their support through fear.

"Power to the People" was one of the most famous slogans used by the Black Panther Party. The phrase represented opposition to the rich, mostly white, ruling class of the United States.

BLACK POWER IN THE LATE 1960s

Between 1966 and 1970, the United States experienced some of the most violent times in its history. Students at colleges from coast to coast were protesting the war in Vietnam. Ironically, communism, which American troops were fighting in Vietnam, was an inspiration to many involved in the Black Power and student movements.

The Black Panthers attracted more members and more attention from law enforcement. J. Edgar Hoover, head of the FBI, called the Black Panther Party the "greatest threat to the internal security of the country." During this time, there were multiple police raids in various cities aimed at ending the Black Panther Party. After a 1967 shoot-out with police, Huey Newton, cofounder of the Black Panthers, was wounded and arrested and charged for the death of a police officer. He was found guilty of involuntary manslaughter. His case was overturned in 1970. Chicago Black Panther Party chapter leader Fred Hampton was shot in his bed as he slept during a raid.

The Black Panthers almost immediately attracted the attention of law enforcement. Throughout the 1960s and '70s, the FBI considered them a radical political group and spent years trying to discredit and destroy them.

BLACK POWER IN THE 1970s

Although black culture and Black Power were experiencing a high point in the 1970s, the economic status of the black community was not. Large northern cities continued to become poorer as white residents moved to the suburbs to escape the threat of riots and civil unrest. Sadly, few whites chose to look at the causes of unrest, seeing the violence itself as the cause for poor urban conditions and not the result of them.

The 1970s saw the Black Panthers and newer organizations like the Black Liberation Party launching more attacks on law enforcement and government. This violence came with a price for the Black Power movement—the loss of much of its white support. Part of this was due to the openly violent

The clothing worn by the Black Panthers was one of the most recognizable images of the late 1960s and 1970s. The black berets were chosen to contrast the green berets worn by American soldiers.

statements made by the Black Panthers. Additionally, many black organizations began to adopt a much less multicultural stance and stopped working with white radical groups.

THE DECLINE OF BLACK POWER

The Black Panthers closed many of their chapters by the mid-1970s and many of the leaders relocated to Oakland, the site of the first Black Panther chapter. These years marked a shift in the Black Panther philosophy. The group's leadership decided to enter politics in order to make a change from inside the system. This had already been happening due to the Black Power movement. By 1975, almost three thousand black Americans held elected offices in United States, including in Congress. This was a far cry from the one hundred office-holders in 1964.

This involvement in mainstream society caused a divide in the Black Panther Party. Although Huey Newton and others wanted to use the political process to their advantage, others

The message of the Black Panthers was not only heard by African Americans. Whites from other political groups were sometimes allied with the BPP against discrimination and the Vietnam War.

still wanted to remain outside the system and cause change through revolution. This split resulted in violence between the two groups and accelerated the decline of the Black Panther Party and the Black Power movement.

THE END OF BLACK POWER

By the 1980s, many of the original leaders of the Black Power movement were either dead or imprisoned. Black Panther membership had declined. The original goals of the Black Panther Party had given way to violent acts without a philosophy. In the words of former Black Panther spokesman Eldridge Cleaver, "As it was [the US government] chopped off the head [of the Black liberation movement] and left the body there armed. That's why all these young bloods are out there now, they've got the rhetoric but are without the political direction ... and they've got the guns."

The New Black Panther Party was formed in 1989, an organization not endorsed by former members of the Black Panther Party. Today, both the Southern Poverty Law Center (SPLC) and members of the original Black Panther Party consider the New Black Panther Party a hate group.

The Southern Poverty Law Center describes the New Black Panther Party as "a virulently racist and anti-Semitic organization whose leaders have encouraged violence against whites, Jews, and law enforcement officers."

BEYOND BLACK POWER

By 1990, the Black Power movement was virtually in ruins except in one area: music. Afrocentrism and multiculturalism were kept alive by this energetic art form. In the words of the rapper Chuck D, "Rap music is the invisible TV station that black America never had."

Much of the music that rappers and DJs used as backgrounds to their lyrics was a huge part of the soundtrack to the Black Power movement. Today, echoes of the ideas behind Black Power can still be heard in rap and hip-hop.

During the 1990s, hip-hop became one of the most popular forms of music in the world. Like the Black Power movement before it, different viewpoints and attitudes came

The art of rapping has its roots in the poetry and spoken word performances of the 1960s. The message has often been one of strength and resistance to oppression.

together in hip-hop to present a picture of what was happening in African American communities. Some musicians were violent, and some were peaceful, but they all had the same vision: fair treatment and social and economic justice for African Americans.

BLACK POWER TODAY

Today, racial justice is still needed. Groups like Black Lives Matter (BLM) have chosen nonviolent protest over revolution to bring attention to the unjust killings of black Americans. Separating myth from truth in the history of Black Power and the Black Panthers can be difficult. The terrible violence committed by some people and groups associated with Black Power often overshadows the reasons that led to the movement's start.

The fiftieth anniversary of the Black Power movement came in 2016. This movement is an important part of American history and it teaches us the lesson that when people are

Black Lives Matter and other groups of this millennium have come full circle, embracing the nonviolent protest of the civil rights movement over violence against the establishment.

abused and treated unfairly, they may choose violence if they feel they have no other options. Films like 2011's *The Black Power Mixtape 1967–1969* are helping people understand that the tale of the Black Power movement is complex and still evolving.

GLOSSARY

Afrocentric Focusing on African American history and culture.

assassination The murder of a leader or ruler for political or religious reasons.

black nationalism A movement that believes in separation of black and white Americans.

civil rights The rights of freedom, equality, and equal opportunity citizens have in a society.

civil unrest Violence caused by citizens of a city or country.

hate group An organization that supports or uses violence or hatred against people of different ethnicities, religions, or genders.

infiltrate To sneak into a group or organization to get secret information.

intimidate To bully someone into taking an action against his or her will.

Jim Crow Strict laws passed in the southern United States after the Civil War that segregated African Americans from white society.

militant Willing to be violent to achieve a political goal.

prejudice A negative opinion made without facts or research.

Reconstruction The period of time (1865–1867) after the Civil War during which government officials worked to rebuild the South and right the wrongs of the era of slavery.

retaliate To fight back.

segregation Setting a particular group of people apart based on race or gender.

self-determination The ability to live how one wants without outside influence.

sit-in A type of protest that involves peacefully sitting or standing in a place until needs or desires are addressed.

slavery The ownership of people by other people for the purpose of unpaid labor without freedom.

California African American Museum
600 State Drive - Exposition Park
Los Angeles, CA 90037
(213) 744-7432
Website: http://www.caamuseum.org
Facebook: @CAAMinLA
Twitter: @CAAMinLA
The museum seeks "to research, collect, preserve, and interpret for public enrichment the history, art and culture of African Americans."

Chatham-Kent Black Historical Society
177 King Street East
Inside the WISH Centre
Chatham, ON N7M 3N1
Canada
(519) 352-3565
Website: https://ckbhs.org
Facebook: @CKBHS
Twitter: @CKBHS94
Instagram: @ckblackhistoricalsociety
This nonprofit organization is dedicated to the black history of the city of Chatham, Ontario, and nearby areas.

National Civil Rights Museum (NCRM)
450 Mulberry Street
Memphis, TN 38103
(901) 521-9699
Website: https://www.civilrightsmuseum.org
Facebook: @NCRMuseum
Instagram: @ncrMuseum

Twitter: @NCRMuseum
The museum's exhibits tell the story of the Black Power movement.

National Museum of African American History & Culture
14th Street and Constitution Avenue
Washington, DC 20001
(844) 750-3012
Website: https://nmaahc.si.edu
Facebook: @NMAAHC
Instagram: @NMAAHC
Twitter: @NMAAHC
This museum is part of the nineteen museums and galleries that make up the Smithsonian Institution.

Oakland Museum of California (OMCA)
1000 Oak Street
Oakland, CA 94607
(510) 318-8400
Website: http://museumca.org
Facebook: @museumca
Instagram: @oaklandmuseumca
Twitter: @oaklandmuseumca
The OMCA focuses on art, history, and natural sciences.

Websites

Because of the changing nature of internet links, Rosen Publishing has developed an online list of websites related to the subject of this book. This site is updated regularly. Please use this link to access this list:

http://www.rosenlinks.com/SCRM/Unrest

FOR FURTHER READING

Alexander, Michelle. *The New Jim Crow: Mass Incarceration in the Age of Colorblindness.* New York, NY: The New Press, 2010.

Baldwin, James. *The Fire Next Time*. New York, NY: Vintage Books, 1992.

Bausam, Ann. *The March Against Fear: The Last Great Walk of the Civil Rights Movement and the Emergence of Black Power.* Washington, DC: National Geographic Children's Books, 2017.

Carson, Clayborne. *In Struggle: SNCC and the Black Awakening of the 1960s*. New York, NY: Harvard University Press, 1995.

Cleaver, Eldridge. *Soul on Ice.* Crystal Lake, IL: Delta Publishing, 1999.

Coates, Ta-Nehisi. *Between the World and Me*. New York, NY: Spiegel & Grau, 2015.

Ellison, Ralph. *Invisible Man*. New York, NY: Vintage Books, 1995.

Joseph, Peniel E. *Waiting 'Til the Midnight Hour: A Narrative History of Black Power in America*. New York, NY: Henry Holt & Co., 2006.

Magloon, Kekla. *Fire in the Streets*. New York, NY: Aladdin Paperbacks, 2013.

Magloon, Kekla. *The Rock and the River*. New York, NY: Aladdin Paperbacks, 2010.

Partridge, Elizabeth. *Marching for Freedom: Walk Together, Children, and Don't You Grow Weary*. New York, NY: Viking Books for Young Readers, 2009.

Saddleback Educational Publishing. *The Civil Rights Movement & Vietnam: 1960–1976*. Costa Mesa, CA: Saddleback Educational Publishing, 2008.

Seale, Bobby. *Power to the People: The World of the Black Panthers*. Photographs by Stephen Shames. New York, NY: Abrams Books, 2016.

Shakur, Asiata, and Angela Davis. *Assata: An Autobiography*. Chicago, IL: Lawrence Hill Books, 2001.

X, Malcolm, and Alex Haley. *The Autobiography of Malcolm X: As Told to Alex Haley.* New York, NY: Ballantine Books, 1987.

BIBLIOGRAPHY

Aretha, David. *Sit-ins and Freedom Rides*. Greensboro, NC: Morgan Reynolds Publishing, 2009.

Baggins, Brian. "*Black Panther Party*." Retrieved March 4, 2017. https://www.marxists.org/history/usa/workers/black-panthers.

Baptist, Edward E. *The Half Has Never Been Told: Slavery and the Making of American Capitalism*. New York, NY: Basic Books, 2014.

Blackmon, Douglas A. *Slavery by Another Name: The Re-Enslavement of Black Americans from the Civil War to World War II*. New York, NY: Doubleday, 2008.

Bloom, Joshua, and Waldo E. Martin Jr. *Black Against Empire: The History and Politics of the Black Panther Party*. Berkeley, CA: University of California Press, 2014.

Bynum, Thomas. *NAACP Youth and the Fight for Black Freedom, 1936–1965*. Knoxville, TN: University of Tennessee Press, 2013.

Carson, Clayborne, et. al. *Eyes on the Prize Civil Rights Reader: Documents, Speeches, and Firsthand Accounts from the Black Freedom Struggle*. New York, NY: Penguin Books, 1991.

Morgan, Iwan, and Philip Davis. *From Sit-ins to SNCC: The Student Civil Rights Movement in the 1960s*. Gainesville, FL: University Press of Florida, 2013.

Seale, Bobby. *Power to the People: The World of the Black Panthers*. Photographs by Stephen Shames. New York, NY: Abrams Books, 2016.

Ture, Kwame, and Charles V. Hamilton. *Black Power: The Politics of Liberation*. New York, NY: Vintage Books, 1992.

Van Deburg, William L. *New Day in Babylon: The Black Power Movement and American Culture*. Chicago, IL: University of Chicago Press, 1992.

Williams, Juan, and Julian Bond. *Eyes on the Prize: America's Civil Rights Years, 1954–1965*. New York, NY: Penguin Books, 2013.

INDEX

ABOUT THE AUTHOR

Kerry Hinton is a writer and DJ who has a keen interest in social justice and civil rights. His parents weren't Black Panthers, but they lived in New York during the turbulent times of the 1960s. Their stories of the Harlem Riots of 1964 and the early days of the Black Power movement have influenced him greatly. He lives in Brooklyn, New York.

PHOTO CREDITS

Cover, pp. 1, 33 David Fenton/Archive Photos/Getty Images; pp. 3, 42, 43, 45, 46, 47 Onur Ersin/Shutterstock.com; pp. 4, 6, 8, 10, 12, 14, 16, 20, 24, 28, 30, 32, 34, 36, 38, 40, back cover Sergey Kamshylin/Shutterstock.com; p. 5 PhotoQuest/Archive Photos /Getty Images; p. 7 Steven Clevenger/Corbis Historical/Getty Images; p. 9 Pictorial Parade/Archive Photos/Getty Images; pp. 11, 25 Bettmann/Getty Images; p. 13 © iStockphoto.com/peeterv; p. 15 Library of Congress Prints and Photographs Division; p. 17 John D. Kisch/Separate Cinema Archive/Archive Photos/Getty Images; p. 18 Time Life Pictures/The LIFE Images Collection/Getty Images; pp. 21, 26 Ted Streshinsky Photographic Archive/Corbis Historical /Getty Images; pp. 22–23 Garofalo Jack/Paris Match Archive /Getty Images; p. 29 David Frent/Corbis Historical/Getty Images; p. 31 © iStockphoto.com/mixmotivew; p. 35 Robert Altman /Archive Photos/Getty Images; p. 37 Scott Olson/Getty Images; p. 39 hurricanehank/Shutterstock.com; p. 41 John Gomez /Shutterstock.com.

Designer: Nelson Sá; Editor and Photo Researcher: Xina M. Uhl